it was a little girl.

Hee Haw!

She was so cute and small!

She was a **dinky** donkey.

Wonky Donkey had a child,
it was a little girl.

Hee Haw!

She was so cute and small . . .

and she had beautiful *long* eyelashes!

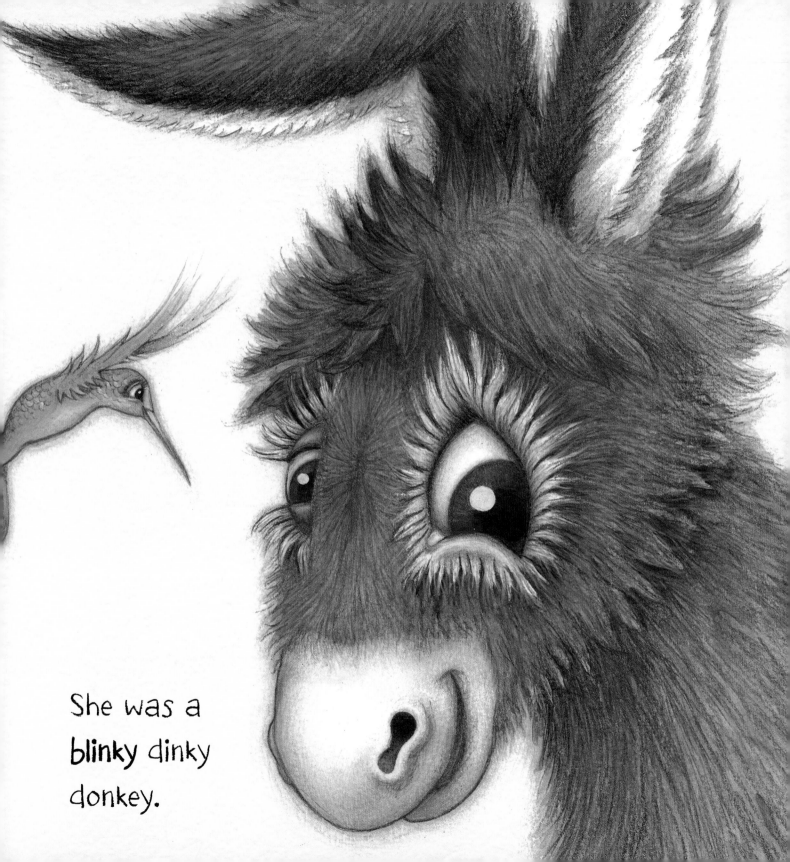

She was a
blinky dinky
donkey.

Wonky Donkey had a child,
it was a little girl.

Hee Haw!

She was so cute and small,
she had beautiful long eyelashes . . .

and she loved to listen to rowdy music.

She was a **punky** blinky dinky donkey.

Wonky Donkey had a child,
it was a little girl.

Hee Haw!

She was so cute and small,
she had beautiful long eyelashes,
she loved to listen to rowdy music . . .

and she painted her hooves bright pink.

She was an
inky-pinky
punky
blinky
dinky donkey.

Wonky Donkey had a child,
it was a little girl.

Hee Haw!

She was so cute and small,
she had beautiful long eyelashes,
she loved to listen to rowdy music,
she painted her hooves bright pink . . .

and she had to go pee-pee.

She was a **winky-tinky** inky-pinky
punky blinky dinky donkey.

Wonky Donkey had a child,
it was a little girl.

Hee Haw!

She was so cute and small,
she had beautiful long eyelashes,
she loved to listen to rowdy music,
she painted her hooves bright pink,
she had to go pee-pee . . .

and she loved to play the piano.

She was a **plinky-plonky** winky-tinky inky-pinky punky blinky dinky donkey.

Wonky Donkey had a child,
it was a little girl.

Hee Haw!

She was so cute and small,
she had beautiful long eyelashes,
she loved to listen to rowdy music,
she painted her hooves bright pink,
she had to go pee-pee,
she loved to play the piano . . .

and she wore wild sunglasses.

She was a **funky** plinky-plonky winky-tinky
inky-pinky punky blinky dinky donkey.

Wonky Donkey had a child,
it was a little girl.

Hee Haw!

She was so cute and small,
she had beautiful long eyelashes,
she loved to listen to rowdy music,
she painted her hooves bright pink,
she had to go pee-pee,
she loved to play the piano,
she wore wild sunglasses . . .

**and she smelt just as bad
as her dad.**

She was a **stinky** funky plinky-plonky winky-tinky inky-pinky punky blinky dinky donkey.

Wonky Donkey had a child,
it was a little girl . . .